This book is intended to provide children with a sense of place—a constant, familiar place to return to time and again. While exploring Crinkle Cove, children learn how living things find their own place within the larger environment. Understanding the sense of home even a small area can provide a wild creature is the first step in gaining a wider appreciation of nature as a whole. With today's important world-wide environmental concerns being discussed in classrooms and on TV, Crinkle Cove gives a child a worry-free rest, a safe, secure place to come home to and nestle down in for a while.

Jim Arnosky

To Ryan and Tyler

First Aladdin Paperbacks edition October 1999

Text and illustrations copyright © 1998 by Jim Arnosky

Aladdin Paperbacks
An imprint of Simon & Schuster Children's Publishing Division
1230 Avenue of the Americas
New York, NY 10020

Also available in a Simon & Schuster Books for Young Readers hardcover edition.
Book design by Heather Wood and Jim Arnosky.
The text for this book was set in Cantoria.

A NOTE ABOUT THE ART IN THIS BOOK: These illustrations were created with acrylic paints
using both transparent and opaque washes.

Printed and bound in Hong Kong
10 9 8 7 6 5 4 3 2 1

The Library of Congress has cataloged the hardcover edition as follows:
Arnosky, Jim.
Crinkleroot's visit to Crinkle Cove / story and pictures by Jim Arnosky.
p.   cm.
Summary: Crinkleroot searches for his friend, a small orange snake, through a soggy shoreland woods to
the lake, under lily pads, and on a grassy knoll full of frogs, examining the animals and plants along the way.
ISBN 0-689-81602-2
[1. Lake ecology—Fiction. 2. Ecology—Fiction. 3. Snakes—Fiction.] I. Title.
PZ7.A7384Cr   1998   [E]—dc21   97-39456
ISBN 0-689-81603-0 (Aladdin pbk.)

Crinkleroot's
VISIT TO
CRINKLE COVE

ALADDIN PAPERBACKS

Hello! My name is Crinkleroot. I live here in the woods.

Have you seen a small orange snake? Her name is Sassafrass, and she's my friend.

I've been looking through the forest for her. Just yesterday she was coiled on my hat, soaking in the sun. Then she went exploring, and I haven't seen her since.

Walking Stick, where do you think Sassafrass went?

Do you think she's in the pine forest? Or the wildflower valley? How about the lake? That's it! I think she's at the lake, and I know just the spot to look.

It's a special place called Crinkle Cove where the water always sparkles and cattails wave in the gentle breeze. There's a dock for swimming, a boat for rowing, and a wishing well for, well . . . wishing!

Look, here's Sassafrass' trail. Let's follow it.

There's my old fishing shack, which I use as a workshop to build birdhouses. I'll bet Sassafrass is inside. She has her own entrance. Can you spot it?

Sassafrass likes the woody smell of the unfinished nest boxes. She's especially fond of wren boxes. She enjoys squeezing through the tiny wren-sized entrance holes.

This is 1″ diameter

Wrens don't care what their houses look like as long as the entrance hole is no larger than one inch wide.

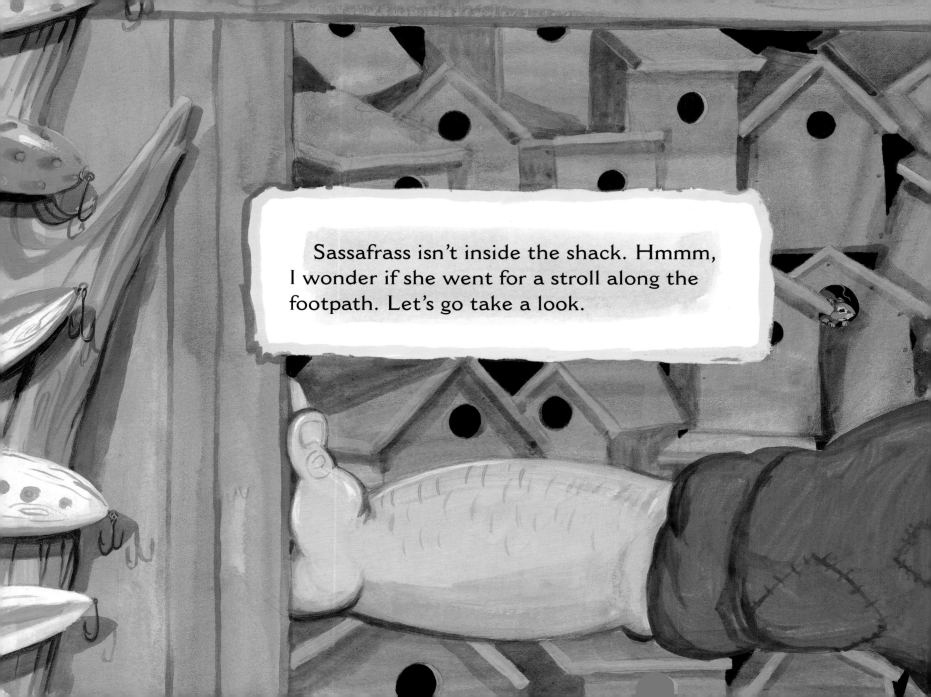

Sassafrass isn't inside the shack. Hmmm, I wonder if she went for a stroll along the footpath. Let's go take a look.

Yes! Sassafrass was here. I see her trail. Do you?

The footpath at Crinkle Cove winds through soggy woods and ends up at the cattails that grow along the water's edge.

There are a lot of things in the wet woods for Sassafrass to see.

Raccoon and deer tracks are pressed in the soft woods soil.

There's a wonderfully woven oriole nest hanging from a maple limb.

And in the lowest spots, where the lake water seeps in, muskrats swim between the trees looking for sweet green ferns to eat.

I can see why Sassafrass' trail led here. What a lovely view of the lake! The great blue heron is in Cattail Corner. Herons wade slowly in the shallow water, looking for small fish to eat.

I'm surprised Sassafrass isn't here, coiled on this tree root. She loves watching the heron catch fish.

While we're here, let's wade in the shallow water and peek under the lily pads. Maybe Sassafrass is hiding there.

Whoops! That's not Sassafrass! That's a large-mouth bass! Sassafrass wouldn't go swimming where such big fish could gobble her up. She must have gone someplace else.

Maybe we'll see Sassafrass along the water's edge. She comes here to play. Sassafrass uses her nose to push pretty shoreline stones into nice, neat piles.

Crinkle Cove ⚓

At Crinkle Cove, every stone is a different color.

There are red stones
(sandstone)

and blue stones.
(blue sandstone)

There are stones with zebra stripes.
(white quartz in black shale)

How many different colored stones can you find on your next walk? See how high you can pile them.

Look here! It's the tiny miner's hat Sassafrass wears when she goes exploring after dark.

This grassy knoll is full of frogs. Sassafrass must have come last night to count frogs! Let's see, one frog, two, three . . .

How many frogs do you see?

There she is, napping in the boat. Sassafrass! It's me, Crinkleroot. Walking Stick and I have been looking for you.

Now that we're together, let's row back to Cattail Corner and then we can take the footpath to the shack. We could paint a birdhouse or make a wish at the well. We always have such a good time at Crinkle Cove. I wish we could come here every day.

CRINKLE COVE